Mel Bay Presents

A Treasury of S ... for Young People

for Autoharp,
Guitar, Ukulele, Mandolin, Banjo, and Keyboard

Compiled and Arranged by Meg Peterson

MEL BAY ®

1 2 3 4 5 6 7 8 9 0

Visit us on the Web at www.melbay.com — E-mail us at email@melbay.com

Preface

The songs in this book have been chosen because of their familiarity and popularity. They have been arranged in keys that are most suitable for singing, and can be played using only the words and the accompanying chords. In some cases there is more than one version of a particular tune. If both versions are well known, I have included both. If not, I have selected the one that is most widely used. These songs may be played on any instrument capable of chords, ie. guitar, banjo, ukulele, mandolin, keyboard, etc...

I have arranged the songs for the 15 and 21 chord standard Autoharp. Those who have diatonic or specially made instruments will be able to adapt the arrangements by transposing the melodies to a different key as explained in *Mel Bay's Complete Method for Autoharp or Chromoharp.** The songs are also chorded for a variety of styles, from simple strumming (few chords) to melody picking (more frequent chord changes).* You can hear the melody emerge as you vary your stroke and play in the different areas (octaves) of the Autoharp.

A slash (/) means to repeat the chord in the rhythm of the song until a new chord is indicated. Slashes also indicate the rhythmic pattern of the piece. When there are several slashes over one word, the strokes will naturally be shorter and the tempo (speed) will be faster. These slashes can be varied and will help make your playing more interesting, whether it's accompaniment or a melody solo. You may add or subtract slashes as you perfect your own style. They are merely guidelines and need not be followed rigidly.

A quarter rest (𝄽) means that you do not sing on that beat. Sometimes you will stroke a chord on it, and other times you will remain silent.

A repeat sign (:‖) means to repeat the previous verse or phrase.

D.C. is an abbreviation for Da Capo, which means "from the beginning."

Fine means the end.

D.C. al Fine means to go back to the beginning of the song and play to *Fine*.

(𝄾) means *Arpeggiando*,* a slow, gentle stroke from the lower to the higher octave.

A chord is put in parentheses if it is not essential to the harmony, but just adds color to the arrangement. If you do not have that particular chord on your Autoharp, just continue playing the previous one. Or, in some cases, I have used a chord that is only on the 21 chord instrument, and put the 15 chord substitute in parentheses.

The Treasury of Songs series has been designed with clarity and convenience in mind. If you play your Autoharp on your lap or place it on a table, you can fold back the book to the desired page and insert it between the two rows of tuning pins on the slanted side of the instrument. The songs will then be in full view and both hands will be free for playing. I hope you and your friends and family will use this collection of songs to enrich your time together and utilize the Autoharp as the versatile, exciting instrument that it is.

Happy Strumming!

Meg Peterson

Maplewood, NJ

May, 2003

*Mel Bay Publications, Inc., Pacific, MO 63069: transposition, p. 164; simple strums, p. 18-32: melody picking, p.51-80; arpeggiando, p.23

Alphabetical Index of Song Titles

Children's Songs

Baa! Baa! Black Sheep

```
C    /    /    /    F       /    C    /  G7  /   C   /  G7  /    C   /
```
Baa! Baa! Black sheep, have you any wool?   Yes, sir, yes, sir, three bags full;

```
/    /    G7  /      C   /    G7   /     C  /      F     /       C   G7      C
```
One for my mas-ter and one for my dame,   and one for the lit-tle boy who lives down the lane.

Billy Boy

```
C  /    /      /    /    /    /      /
```
Oh, where have you been Billy boy, Billy boy,

```
/    /    /      /    /       G7  / /
```
Oh, where have you been charming Billy?

```
/      /      /    /    /      C  /      /
```
I have been to seek a wife, she's the joy of my life,

```
F    C    /       G7   /      C   / /
```
She's a young thing and cannot leave her mother.

Ring Around the Rosy

```
C    /       / / /    /      / / / / /    /    G7 /  C    /
```
Ring a-round the ros-y, a pocket full of po-sies, ash-es, ash-es, we all   fall down!

Kum By Yah

```
C    /    /    / F    C // /      /      / / F      G7 // 
```
Kum by yah, my Lord,   Kum by yah,   Kum by yah, my Lord,   Kum by yah,

```
C    /    / / F    C // F  C  / G7    C // 
```
Kum by yah, my Lord,   Kum by yah.   Oh, Lord,   Kum by yah.

2. Someone's praying, my Lord, Kum by yah, someone's praying, my Lord, Kum by yah,
Someone's praying, my Lord, Kum by yah. Oh, Lord,   Kum by yah.

3. Someone's crying, my Lord, Kum by yah, Someone's crying, my Lord, Kum by yah,
Someone's crying, my Lord, Kum by yah. Oh, Lord,   Kum by yah

---

The Fox

```
   C    /    /    /      /        /      G7      / 
```
The fox went out on a chilly night, and he prayed to the moon for to give him light,

```
   C    / F    /      C  G7      C  / G7 / C  / 
```
For he'd many a mile to go that night, Be—fore he reached the town, oh, town, oh, town, oh;

```
F    /    C    /      G7    /        C    / 
```
He'd many a mile to go that night Be—fore he reached the town, oh.

2. He ran till he came to a great big pen, Where the ducks and the geese were kept therein,
A couple of you will grease my chin Before I leave this town, oh, town, oh, town, oh,
A couple of you will grease my chin Before I leave this town, oh.

3. He grabbed the gray goose by the neck, throwed a duck across his back,
He didn't mind the quack, quack, quack, and the legs all dangling down, oh, down, oh, down, oh,
He didn't mind the quack, quack, quack, and the legs all dangling down, oh.

4. Then old Mrs. Flipper-Flopper jumped out of bed, out of the window she cocked her head,
Saying, "John, John, the goose is gone, and the fox is on the town, oh, town, oh, town, oh."
Saying, "John, John, the goose is gone, and the fox is on the town, oh."

5. Then John he ran to the top of the hill, blowed his horn both loud and shrill.
Fox, he said, "I'd better flee with my kill, for they'll soon be on my trail, oh, trail, oh, trail, oh,"
Fox, he said, "I'd better flee with my kill, for they'll soon be on my trail, oh."

Father's Whiskers

F / / / **G7** / / /
I have a dear old daddy,   for whom I nightly pray;

C7 / / / / / **F**
He has a set of whiskers that are always in the way.

Chorus:
C7 **F** / / / **G7** / / /
They're always in the way,   the cows eat them for hay,

C7 / / / / / **F**
They hide the dirt on Father's shirt, they're always in the way.

2. I have a dear old mother, with him at night she sleeps.
She wakes up in the morning, eating shredded wheat. *Chorus*

3. Around the supper table, we make a happy group,
Until dear Father's whiskers get tangled in the soup. *Chorus*

4. When Father goes out swimming, no bathing suit for him;
He wraps his whiskers 'round him, and gaily plunges in. *Chorus*

Hey, Lolly, Lolly

Chorus:
D / / / / / **A7** /
⅔ Hey, lol—ly, lol—ly, lol—ly, ⅔ hey, lol—ly, lol—ly, lo—

/ / / / / / **D** /
⅔ Hey, lol—ly, lol—ly, lol—ly, ⅔ hey, lol—ly, lol—ly, lo.

1. I may be right and I may be wrong,   ⅔ hey, lol—ly, lol—ly, lo—
But I know you're gonna sing this song, ⅔ hey, lol—y, lol—ly, lo. *Chorus*

2. I know a girl who's ten feet tall,⅔ hey, lol–ly, lol–ly, lo—
Sleeps in the kitchen with her feet in the hall; ⅔ hey, lol–ly, lol–ly, lo. *Chorus*

3. Everybody sing the chorus, ⅔ hey, lol–ly, lol–ly, lo—
Either you're against us or you're for us, ⅔ hey, lol–ly, lol–ly, lo. *Chorus*

4. The purpose of this little song, ⅔ hey, lol–ly, lol–ly, lo—
Is to make up verses as you go along, ⅔hey, lol–ly, lol–ly, lo. *Chorus*

Mary Had a Little Lamb

```
F    /   /   /   C7  /   F   /   /   /   /   /      C7      /      F   /
```
Mary had a little lamb, little lamb, little lamb, Mary had a little lamb, its fleece was white as snow.

2. And every where that Mary went, Mary went, Mary went
Everywhere that Mary went, the lamb was sure to go.

3. He followed her to school one day, school one day, school one day,
He followed her to school one day, which was against the rules.

4. It made the children laugh and play, laugh and play, laugh and play,
   It made the children laugh and play to see a lamb at school.

Pop Goes the Weasel

```
C   G7    C    /       /    G7      C  /
```
All a-round the cobbler's bench the monkey chased the weas-el

```
   C     G7     C     /   F  G7     C   /
```
The monkey stopped to tie up his shoe. Pop! Goes the weas-el.

```
  Am  D7   G       /        Am  D7   G  /
```
A penny for a spool of thread; A penny for a nee-dle.

```
F          /   /   /   /  G7      C   /
```
That's the way the money goes. Pop! Goes the weas-el.

Old MacDonald Had a Farm

```
F        /    Bb  F  /  C7  F /     /   /      Bb      F   /  C7  F  /
```
Old Mac—Donald had a farm, E, I, E, I, O.   And on his farm he had some chicks, E, I, E, I, O.

```
   F        /      /      /   /     Bb      F      Bb
```
With a chick—chick here, and a chick—chick there; here a chick, there a chick, everywhere a chick—chick,

```
F        /    Bb  F  /  C7  F /
```
Old Mac—Donald had a farm, E, I, E, I, O.

2. Ducks: Quack–quack.
3. Turkeys: Gobble–gobble.
4. Pigs: Oink–oink.
5. Cows: Moo–moo.

London Bridge is Falling Down

C   /   /   /   G7 /   C   /   /   /   /   /   G7 /   C   /
London bridge is falling down, falling down, falling down. London bridge is falling down, my   fair lady.

Skip To My Lou

C   /   /   /   G7   /   /   /
Lost my partner, what'll I do? Lost my partner, what'll I do?

C   /   /   /   G7   /   /   /
Lost my partner, what'll I do? Skip to my Lou, my dar—lin.

Chorus:
C /   /   /   G7 /   /   /
Lou, Lou, skip to my Lou; Lou, Lou, skip to my Lou;

 C /   /   /   G7   /   C /
Lou, Lou, skip to my Lou; Skip to my Lou, my dar—lin.

2. I'll get another one, prettier than you...*Chorus*
3. Flies in the buttermilk, shoo fly, shoo...*Chorus*

Twinkle, Twinkle Little Star

C   /   /   /   F / C / Dm G7 C   Am Dm G7 C /
Twin—kle, twin—kle lit—tle star.   How I won—der what you are.

/ / G7 / C   / G7 / C / G7 /   C D7 G7 /
Up a—bove the world so high,   like a dia—mond in the sky.

C   /   /   /   F / C / Dm G7 C   Am Dm G7 C
Twin—kle, twin—kle lit—tle star.   How I won—der what you are.

Hot Cross Buns

C G7 C   C G7 C   /   /   G7 /   C G7 C
Hot Cross Buns! ♩ Hot Cross Buns! ♩ One a penny, two a penny, Hot Cross Buns! ♩

Lavender's Blue

```
C   /   /   C7  /   /   F   /   /   C   //  F   //  C   /   /   Dm  C   G7  C   //
```
Lav—en—der's blue, dilly, dilly, lav—en—der's green,   When I am king, dilly, dilly, you shall be   queen.

2. Who told you so, dilly dilly, who told you so? It was my heart, dilly, dilly, that told me so.

Ten Little Indians

```
F       /       /       /       G7      /       C7      /
```
One little, two little, three little indians, four little, five little, six little indians,

```
F       /       /       /       C7      /       F       /
```
Seven little, eight little, nine little indians, ten little indian boys and girls.

```
/       /       /       /       G7      /       C7      /
```
Ten little, nine little, eight little indians, seven little, six little, five little indians,

```
F       /       /       /       C7      /       F       /
```
Four little, three little, two little indians, one little indian boy or girl.

Lightly Row

```
C    / /   / G7   /  /   / C  G7  C   G7  C   / / /
```
Light—ly row,   light—ly row,   o'er the glas—sy waves we go.

```
/        / /   / G7     / /   / C  / G7 /   C  ///
```
Smooth—ly glide,   smooth—ly slide,   On the si—lent tide.

```
G7  / /   / /   C  G7 /   C   / /  / /   G7  C  /
```
Let the winds and wa—ters be   min—gled with our mel—o—dy;

```
/   / /   / G7  /  /   / C /  G7  / C   / /
```
Sing and float,   sing and float,   in our lit—tle boat.

Sing a Song of Sixpence

```
C   /   /   /       G7      /   / /   /       /   /   /   C   / /
```
Sing a song of six—pence, a pocket—ful of rye.   Four and twenty black—birds baked in a pie.

```
/       /   / /       G7      /   / /   /       /   /   /   /   /   C   /
```
When the pie was o—pened the birds be—gan to sing.   Wasn't that a dainty dish to set be—fore the king?

Jim Along Josie

| F | / | G7 | C7 | F | / | C7 | F |

Hey jim—a—long, jim along Josie, hey jim—a—long, jim along Jo,

| / | / | G7 | C7 | F | / | C7 | F |

Hey jim—a—long, jim along Josie, hey jim—a—long, jim along Jo.

2. Walk jim—a—long, jim along Josie, walk jim—a—long, jim along Jo, etc.
3. Hop jim—a—long, jim along Josie, hop jim—a—long, jim along Jo, etc.
4. Run jim—a—long, jim along Josie, run jim—a—long, jim along Jo, etc.

Shoo, Fly, Don't Bother Me

| F | / | / | C7 | / | / | / | F |

Shoo, fly, don't bother me, shoo, fly,   don't bother me,

| / | / | / | C7 | / | / | / | F |

Shoo, fly,   don't bother me, for I be—long to some—bo—dy. *(Fine)*

| / | / | / | / | / | | C7 | / |

I feel,   I feel,   I feel like a morn—ing star.

| / | / | / | / | / | | / | F | / |

I feel,   I feel,   I feel like a morn—ing star.   *(D.C. al Fine)*

Lazy Mary

| F | / | / | / | G7 | / | C7 | / |

Lazy Mary, will you get up, will you get up, will you get up?

| F | / | / | / | C7 | / | F | / |

Lazy Mary will you get up? Will you get up to—day?

2. No, Mother, I won't get up, I won't get up, I won't get up.
   No, Mother, I won't get up, I won't get up today.

John Jacob Jingelheimer Schmidt

F / / / C7 / / / / / / / F / / /
John   Jac—ob Jingel—heimer Schmidt,   his name   is my name, too.

    / / / / Bb / / /
When—ever we go out   the peo—ple always shout, there goes

C7 / / / F   / C7 /
John Jacob Jingel—heimer Schmidt! Ta da da da da da da...

(Repeat song, singing each verse more quietly until you're only moving your lips.)

Go In and Out the Windows

  F / C7 / / / F   /
Go in and out the windows,   go in and out the windows,

  / / C7 / / / F /
Go in and out the windows,   as we have done be—fore.

Pick a Bale of Cotton

  C7 F   /   Bb   C7
You gotta' jump down, turn a—round, pick a bale of cot—ton

  F   /   C7   F
Oh, jump down, turn a—round, pick a bale a day. :|| *

F / Bb   C7   F / C7   F
Oh, Lordy, pick a bale of cot—ton; oh, Lordy, pick a bale a day.

Oh, Where Has My Little Dog Gone?

  F   /   C7   / C7   /   F /
Oh, where, oh where has my lit—tle dog gone? Oh, where, oh where can he be?

  F   /   C7 / C7   /   F /
WIth his ears cut short and his tail cut long, oh, where, oh where can he be?

Whenever you see this sign (:||), repeat the previous phrase.

Oh, Dear, What Can the Matter Be?

C G7 C /   G7 / /   /
Oh, dear, what can the mat—ter be? Dear, dear, what can the mat—ter be?

C G7 C /   F   G7   C /
Oh, dear, what can the mat—ter be? John—ny's so long at the fair.

  C   /   /   /   G7   /   /   /
He prom—ised to bring me a bas—ket of po—sies, a gar—and of lil—ies, a gar—land of ros—es,

  C   /   /   /   F   G7   C /
A lit—tle straw hat and a bunch of blue rib—bons, to tie up my bon—nie brown hair.

Jack and Jill

 G   D7   G D7 G / C G
Jack and Jill went up the hill to fetch a pail of wa—ter;

D7   /   G   /   C   D7 / G
Jack fell down and broke his crown, and Jill came tumbling af—ter.

2. Up Jack got and home did trot as fast as he could ca—per;
They put him to bed and plastered his head with vinegar and brown pa—per.

This Old Man

F   / /   /
This old man, he played one, (two, three, four, five, six)

B♭   /   C7   /
He played knick—knack on my thumb (shoe, knee, door, hive, sticks).

   F   /   /   / C7   /   /   F
With a knick—knack, paddy whack, give a dog a bone. This old man came rolling home.

7. seven; up to heaven.
8. eight; at the gate.
9. nine; on my spine.
10. ten; over again.

Did You Ever See A Lassie

F /   /   /   /   / **C7** /   / **F** /   /   / /   /   /   / / **C7** /   / **F** /
Did you ev—er see a las—sie, a   las—sie, a   las—sie, did you ev—er see a las—sie go this way and that?

/ **C7** /   / **F** /   /   / **C7** /   / **F** /   /   /   / /   /   /   / / **C7** /   / **F**
Go this way and that way, and this way and that way,   did you ev—er see a las—sie go this way and that?

Shortnin' Bread

C   /   /   /   /   /   **G7**   **C**
Three little chil—dren, lying in bed; two were sick and the other 'most dead!

/   /   /   /   /   /   **G7**   **C**
Sent for the doctor and the doc—tor said, "Feed these children on short—nin' bread."

Chorus:
C   /   /   /   /   /   /   **G7** **C**
Mama's little baby loves short—nin', short—nin', Mama's little baby loves short—nin' bread

/   /   /   /   /   /   **G7** **C**
Mama's little baby loves short—nin', short—nin', Mama's little baby loves short—nin' bread.

Oats, Peas, Beans, And Barley Grow

Chorus:
C   **G7**   /   / **F**   /   **G7**   /
Oats, peas, beans, and barley grow, oats, peas, beans, and barley grow,

   C   / /   /   **F**   **G7**   **C**   /
Can you or I or anyone know how oats, peas, beans, and barley grow?

2. First the farmer waters the seeds, stands erect and takes his ease,
He stamps his foot and claps his hands and turns around to view his lands. *Chorus*

3. Next the farmer hoes the weeds, stands erect and takes his ease,
He stamps his foot and claps his hands and turns around to view his lands. *Chorus*

4. Last the farmer harvests his seeds, stands erect and takes his ease,
He stamps his foot and claps his hands, and turns around to view his lands. *Chorus*

Sailing, Sailing

G   /   /   /   C   /   G /
Sail—ing, sail—ing, over the bounding main,

  D7   /   G   Em   A7   /   D7 /
For many a stormy wind shall blow ere Jack comes home a—gain!

G   /   /   /   C   /   G /
Sail—ing, sail—ing over the bounding main,

  C   B7   Em   A7   G   D7   G /
For many a stormy wind shall blow ere Jack comes home a—gain.

Sleep, Baby, Sleep

F   C7   F   /   /   C7   F /
Sleep, baby, sleep!   Thy father guards the sheep,

  B♭   C7   F   /   B♭   C7   F   /
Thy mother shakes the dreamland tree, and from it falls sweet dreams for thee;

/   C7   F / /   C7   F   /
Sleep, baby, sleep!   Sleep, baby, sleep!

Over The River And Through The Woods

C   /   /   /   F   /   C /
Over the river and through the woods to Grandfather's house we go.

  G7   /   C   /   D7   /   G7 /
The horse knows the way to carry the sleigh through the white and drifting snow.

C   /   /   /   F   /   C /
Over the river and through the woods, oh, how the wind does blow!

  F   /   C   Am   C   G7   C /
It stings the toes and bites the nose as over the ground we go.

Jimmy Crack Corn

| Bb | / | / | / | F | / | C7 | / |

When I was young I used to wait on master and hand him his plate,

| Bb | / | / | / | C7 | / | F | / |

And pass the bottle when he got dry, and brush a—way the blue tail fly.

Chorus:

| F | / | C7 | / | / | / | F | / |

Jimmy crack corn and I don't care, Jimmy crack corn and I don't care,

| (F7) | / | Bb | / | C7 | / | F | / |

Jimmy crack corn and I don't care, my mas—ter's gone a—way!

The More We Get Together

| F | / | C7 | F | / | / | C7 | F |

The more we get to-gether, to-gether, to-gether, the more we get to-gether, the happier we'll be.

| C7 | F | C7 | F |

For your friends are my friends, and my friends are your friends,

| / | / | C7 | F |

The more we get to-gether, the happier well be.

Eency Weency Spider

| F | / | / | / | C7 | / | F | / | / | / | / | / | C7 | / | F | / |

Eency weency spi—der went up the wa—ter spout,   down came the rain and washed the spi—der out,

| / | / | / | / | C7 | / | F | C7 | F | / | / | / | C7 | / | F | / |

Out came the sun and dried up all the rain, then the eency weency spi—der went up the spout a—gain.

Pussy Cat, Pussy Cat

| F | / | / | / | C | / | / | / |

Pussy cat, pussy cat, where have you been? I've been to London to visit the Queen.

| F | C7 | F | Bb | / | F | C7 | F |

Pussy cat, pussy cat, what did you there? I frightened a little mouse under her chair.

15

Clementine

```
     F    /  /  /   /   /    / /     /   C7   /
```
In a cav—ern, in a can—yon, exca—va—ting for a mine,

```
  /     /   / /   F  / /    C7  /   /     F   /
```
Dwelt a min—er forty—nin—er and his daugh—ter, Clemen—tine.

Chorus:
```
F     /   /  /    /   /   /    /  /  /     C7   /
```
Oh, my dar—lin', oh, my dar—lin', oh, my dar—lin' Clemen—tine,

```
  /     /  / /      F  / /    C7  /  /       F  /
```
You are lost and gone for—ev—er. Dreadful sor—ry, Clemen—tine.

2. Light she was and like a feather, and her shoes were number nine,
cardboard boxes without topses, sandals were for Clementine. *Chorus*

3. Drove she ducklings to the water every morning just at nine,
hit her foot against a splinter, fell into the foaming brine. *Chorus*

4. Ruby lips above the water blowing bubbles pure and fine.
Alas for me, I was no swimmer, so I lost my Clementine. *Chorus*

Rockabye Baby

```
G           /  /     D7  /        /     G        /
```
Rock—a—bye baby, on the tree—top, when the wind blows, the cradle will rock;

```
/        /    /     C   G     C   G    A7    D7 G
```
When the bough breaks, the cradle will fall, and down will come ba—by, cra—dle and all.

Hickory, Dickory, Dock

```
C    G7   C  /   /    G7   C   /
```
Hickory, dickory, dock. The mouse ran up the clock.

```
   /      C7   F    / G7   /    C   /
```
The clock struck one, the mouse ran down. Hickory, dickory, dock.

Go Tell Aunt Rhody

Chorus:

C /   /   / G7 /   C   /   /   /   /   / G7   /   C   /

Go tell Aunt Rho—dy, go tell Aunt Rho—dy, go tell Aunt Rho—dy the old gray goose is dead.

2. The one that she's been saving (three times) to make a feather bed. *Chorus*
3. The gander is weeping (three times) because his wife is dead. *Chorus*
4. The goslings are crying (three times) because their mother's dead. *Chorus*
5. She died in the mill pond (three times), the old gray goose is dead. *Chorus*

She'll Be Comin' 'Round The Mountain

C7   F   /   /   /   / ///   /   /   /   /   C7 //

She'll be comin' 'round the mountain when she comes, she'll be comin' 'round the mountain when she comes,

/   F   /   F7   /   Bb   /   /

She'll be comin' 'round the mountain, she'll be comin' 'round the mountain,

/   F   /   C7   /   F   //

She'll be comin' 'round the mountain when she comes.

2. She'll be drivin' six white horses when she comes...
3. Oh, we'll all go out to meet her when she comes...
4. Oh, we'll kill the old red rooster when she comes...
5. And we'll all have chicken and dumplings when she comes...

Michael Finnegan

     F   /   /   /   G7   /   C7   /

There was an old man named Michael Finnegan. He had whiskers on his chinnegan,

     F   /   /   /   C7   /   F   /

The wind blew them off and they grew in again, poor old Michael Finnegan. Begin again.

2. There was an old man named Michael Finnegan. He went fishing with a pinnegan,
Caught a fish and dropped it in again, poor old Michael Finnegan. Begin again.

3. There was an old man named Michael Finnegan. He grew fat and then grew thin again.
Then he died and had to begin again, poor old Michael Finnegan. Begin again.

Froggie Went A-Courtin'

```
  F              /        Bb   C7    //      //
```
A froggie went a—courtin', and he did ride, m—mm, m—mm,

```
  F           /        /     /
```
A froggie went a—courtin', and he did ride,

```
  F          /    /    C7      F/    //
```
A sword and a pistol by his side, m—mm, m–mm.

2. He went to Missy Mousie's door, m—mm, m—mm, etc.
He gave a loud shout and he gave a loud roar, m—mm, m—mm.

3. He said, "Miss Mousie are you within?", m—mm, m—mm, etc.
"Yes, kind sir, I sit and spin," m—mm, m—mm.

4. He took Miss Mousie on his knee, m—mm, m—mm, etc.
He said, "Miss Mousie will you marry me?" m—mm, m—mm.

5. "I'll have to ask Uncle Rat," she said, m—mm, m—mm, etc.
Uncle Rat just smiled and nodded his head, m—mm, m—mm.

6. Now what will the wedding breakfast be? m—mm, m—mm, etc.
Three green beans and a black-eyed pea, m—mm, m—mm.

7. Now when they all sat down to sup, m—mm, m—mm, etc.
A big gray goose came and gobbled them up, m—mm, m—mm.

8. Now that was the end of one, two, three, m—mm, m—mm, etc.
The rat, and the mouse, and the little Froggie, m—mm, m—mm.

9. There's bread and cheese upon the shelf, m—mm, m—mm, etc.
If you want any more you can sing it yourself, m—mm, m—mm.

The Muffin Man

```
  F    /    /    /    G7   /    C7    /
```
Oh, do you know the muffin man, the muffin man, the muffin man,

```
  F    /    /    /    Bb   C7   F    /
```
Oh, do you know the muffin man, who lives in Drury Lane?

Looby Loo

Chorus:

F   /   / / /   /   C7 / F   /   / / C7   /   F   /
Here we go loo-by loo.   Here we go loo-by lignt.   Here we go loo-by loo,   all on a Saturday night.

F   /   / / /   /   / / /   /   /   /
1. I put my right hand in,   I take my right hand out,   I give my right hand a shake, shake, shake,

/   C7   F /
And turn my-self a-bout. *Chorus*

2. I put my left hand in, etc.
3. I put my right foot in, etc.
4. I put my left foot in, etc.
5. I put my whole head in, etc.
6. I put my whole self in, etc.

The Mulberry Bush

F   /   /   /   G7   /   C7   /
Here we go 'round the mulberry bush, the mulberry bush, the mulberry bush,

F   /   /   /   C7 / F   /
Here we go 'round the mulberry bush, so early in the morn—ing.

2. This is the way we brush our teeth...
3. This is the way we wash our clothes...
4. This is the way we iron our clothes...
5. This is the way we go to school...

Goober Peas

G /   /   / C /   G / /   /   / / Am   /   D7 /
Sitting by the road—side on a summer's day,   chatting with my mess–mates, passing time away.

G /   /   / C   /   G / /   /   C   / G D7 G /
Lying in the shadow   under—neath the tree;   goodness how delicious, eating goober peas.

/   / C / D7 /   G / /   /   C   / G D7 G /
Peas! Peas! Peas! Peas! Eating goober peas.   Goodness how delicious   eating goober peas.

Paw Paw Patch

F   /   /   /   **G7**   /   **C7**   /
Where, oh where, is dear little Susie? Where, oh where, is dear little Susie?

F   /   /   /   **C7**   /   **F**   /
Where, oh where, is dear little Susie? Way down yonder in the paw paw patch.

Refrain:
F   /   /   /   **C7**   /   /   /
Pickin' up paw paws, put 'em in the basket, pickin' up paw paws, put 'em in the basket,

F   /   /   /   **C7**   /   **F**   /
Pickin' up paw paws, put 'em in the basket, way down yonder in the paw paw patch.

2. Come on, boys, let's go find her, come on, boys, let's go find her,
Come on, boys, let's go find her, way down yonder in the paw paw patch. *Refrain*

Blow The Man Down

C   /   /   /   /   **A7**   **Dm**   **G7**
Come all ye young fellows who follow the sea, to me way! Hey! Blow the man down.

    /   /   /   /   /   **C**   /
Now pray pay at-tention and listen to me, give me some time to blow the man down.

Rig-A-Jig-Jig

C   /   /   /   **G7**   /   **C**   /
As I was walking down the street, down the street, down the street,

   /   /   /   /   **G7**   /   **C** /
A pretty girl (handsome boy) I chanced to meet, heigh ho, heigh ho, heigh ho.

Refrain:
C   /   /   /   **G7**   /   **C**   /
Rig—a—jig—jig and a—way we go, a—way we go, a—way we go,

/   /   /   /   **G7**   /   **C** /
Rig-a-jig-jig and a—way we go, heigh ho, heigh ho, heigh ho.

Drunken Sailor

Dm / / / **C** / / /
What shall we do with a drunken sailor? What shall we do with a drunken sailor?

Dm / / / / **C** **Dm** /
What shall we do with a drunken sailor, earlye in the morn—ing.

Refrain:
Dm / / / **C** / / / **Dm** / / / / **C** **Dm** /
Way heigh and up she rises, way heigh and up she rises, way heigh and up she rises, earlye in the morn—ing.

2. Put him in a long boat til he's sober. (3 x) Earlye in the morning. *Refrain*
3. Pull out the plug and wet him all over. (3x) Earlye in the morning. *Refrain*
4. Put him in the scuppers with a hose pipe on him. (3x) Earlye in the morning. *Refrain*
5. Shave his belly with a rusty razor. (3x) Earlye in the morning. *Refrain*
6. Heave him by the leg in a runnin' bowlin'. (3x) Earlye in the morning. *Refrain*

Hush, Little Baby

F / **C7** / / / **F** /
Hush, little ba—by don't say a word, Momma's gonna' buy you a mocking bird.

/ / **C7** / / / **F** /
If that mocking bird won't sing, Momma's gonna buy you a diamond ring.

2. If that diamond ring turns brass, Momma's gonna buy you a looking glass.
If that looking glass gets broke, Momma's gonna buy you a billy goat.

3. If that Billy goat won't pull, Momma's gonna buy you a cart and bull.
If that cart and bull turns over, Momma's gonna buy you a dog named Rover.

4. If that dog named Rover won't bark, Momma's gonna buy you and horse and cart.
If that horse and cart break down, you'll still be the prettiest baby in town.

The Farmer in the Dell

D / / / / / / / / / / / / **A7** **D** /
The farmer in the dell, the farmer in the dell, Heigh, ho, the derry, oh, the farmer in the dell.

Old Dan Tucker

G   /   /   /   /   /   C   D7
Went to town the other night, to hear a noise and see a fight.

G   /   /   /   /   /   D7   G
All the people were running a—round, crying, "Old Dan Tucker's come to town."

Chorus:
G   / C   /   D7   /   /   G
Get out the way, Old Dan Tucker. You're too late to get your supper,

/   /   C   /   D7   /   /   G
Supper's over and dinner's cookin', Old Dan Tucker just standin' there lookin'.

2. Now Old Dan Tucker was a mighty man, he washed his face in a frying pan,
Combed his hair with a wagon wheel, an' died with a toothache in his heel. *Chorus*

New River Train

Chorus:
      F   / / / / // C7 F   /   / / C7 //
Oh, I'm ridin' on that new riv-er train,   Oh, I'm ridin' on that new riv-er train,

/   F / / (F7) B7   // /   C7 / / / F //
It's the same old train that brought me here, gonna' carry me back a - gain

1. Oh, my darlin', you can't love one, Oh, my darlin', you can't love one,
Oh, you can't love one and have any fun, Darlin', you can't love one. (Chorus)

2. Oh, my darlin', you can't love two, Oh, my darlin', you can't love two,
Oh, you can't love two and still be true, Darlin', you can't love two. (Chorus)

Susie, Little Susie

C   /   G7   C   /   /   G7   C
Susie, little Susie, pray what is the news! The geese are going barefoot be—cause they've no shoes,

  G7   C   G7   C   /   /   G7   C
The cobbler has leather but no last to use and so he cannot make them a new pair of shoes.

Big Rock Candy Mountain

   C   G7   C   G7 C G7   C   /
On a summer's day in the month of May a burly bum came hiking

      /   G7   C   G7   C   G7 C   /
Down a shady lane through the sugar cane, he was looking for his liking.

  G7   /   C   /   G7   /   C   /
As he strolled a—long he sang this song, of the land of milk and honey,

      /   G7 C   G7   C   G7 C
Where a bum can stay for many a day, and he won't need any money.

Chorus:
G7——C   /   /   /   F /   C   /
Oh, the buzzin' of the bees in the cigarette trees, the soda water fountain

  G7   /   C   /   G7   / C   /
By the lemonade springs where the bluebird sings, in the Big Rock Candy Mountain.

Jenny Jenkins

  F   /   B♭   C7   F   /   C7 /
Oh, will you wear white, oh my dear, oh my dear, oh, will you wear white, Jenny Jen—kins?

F   (F7)   B♭   C7
I won't wear white 'cause the color's too bright.

Refrain:
  F   /   /   /   B♭ /   /   F
I'll buy me a fol-de-rol-de-til-de-tol-de-seek-a double roll——Jenny Jenkins roll.

2. Oh, will you wear blue? I can't wear blue, it's the color of my shoe. *Refrain*
3. Oh, will you wear red? I can't wear red, it's the color of my head. *Refrain*
   (Fill in with colors until the final verse.)

Final verse:
Then what will you wear, oh my dear, oh my dear, Oh, what will you wear, Jenny Jenkins?
I've nothing to wear, so I'll just go bare. *Refrain*

Mister Rabbit

F   /   /   /   /   /   /   /   /

Mr. Rabbit, Mr. Rabbit, your ears are mighty long. Yes, in—deed, they're put on wrong.

Refrain:
/   /   /   **C7**   **F**   /   /   /   **C7**   **F**

Ev—ery little soul must shine, shine, shine, ev—ery little soul must shine, shine, shine.

2. Mr. Rabbit, Mr. Rabbit, your coat is mighty gray. Yes, indeed, it's made that way. *Refrain*
3. Mr. Rabbit, Mr. Rabbit, your eyes are mighty red. Yes, indeed, I'm almost dead. *Refrain*
4. Mr. Rabbit, Mr. Rabbit, your tail is mighty white. Yes, indeed, I'm goin' out of sight. *Refrain*

Lil' Liza Jane

C   **G7**   **C**   /   **F**   **C**   /   /   **G7**   **C**   /   **G7**   /   **C**   /

I know a gal that you don't know, Li'l Li—za Jane;   Way down south in Balti-more, Li'l Li—za Jane.

Refrain:
C / **F C** /   /   /   / / **F C G7**   /   **C** /

Oh   E-li-za, Li'l Li—za Jane,   Oh E-li-za, Li'l Li—za Jane.

2. Liza Jane looks good to me, Li'l Liza Jane. Sweetest one I ever did see, Li'l Liza Jane. *Refrain*

Bought Me A Cat (cumulative song with actions)

C   /   /   /   /   /   /   /

Bought me a cat, my cat pleased me, I fed my cat under yonder tree.

/   **G7**   **C G7**   **C**

Cat went fiddle dee dee, fiddle dee dee.

C   /   /   /   /   /   /   /

2. Bought me a hen, my hen pleased me, I fed my hen under yonder tree.

/   /   /   /   **G7**   **C G7**   **C**

Hen went chipsy, chopsy, cat went fiddle dee dee, fiddle dee dee.

3. Duck went slishy, sloshy
4. Goose went honk, honk
5. Dog went bow-wow
6. Sheep went baa, baa
7. Cow went moo, moo
8. Baby went Mommy, Mommy

Rounds

Why Shouldn't My Goose

D /   / /   /   /   / /   /   /   / /   /   / /

Why shouldn't my goose, sing as well as thy goose, when I paid for my goose, twice as much as thou?

①   ②   ③   ④

Make New Friends

F   C7   F   C7   F7   C7   F C7   F C7   F   C7   F   C7   F

Make new friends but keep the old;   One is silver and the oth - er   gold.

①   ②   ③   ④

Row, Row, Row Your Boat

C /   /   /   /   /   /   / /   /   /   /   /   /   C /   /

Row, row, row your boat, gently down the stream;   merrily, merrily, merrily, merrily, life is but a dream.

①   ②   ③   ④

Chairs to Mend

C   /   F C   /   /   / F   C   /   /   /   F   C⁻/

Chairs to mend, old chairs to mend, mack - er - el, fresh mack - er - el, any old rags, any old rags?

①   ②   ③

Little Tom Tinker

C   /   /   /   /   / / / /   / /   /   /   G7   C   /

Little Tom Tinker sat down on a clinker and he be - gan to cry: " Maw!   Maw!"   Poor little innocent guy.

①   ②   ③   ④

Dona Nobis Pacem

F   C   F   /   C B♭   F   / C7 F

Dona Nobis Pacem, Pa—cem Dona Nobis Pa—cem

Three Blind Mice

C G7 C ⓪ C G7 C ⓪ C G7   C ⓪ C G7   C ⓪

Three blind mice, three blind mice. See how they run! See how they run!

①   ②

  C G7   C   G7   C   G7   C   G7

They all ran after the farmer's wife, she cut off their tails with a carving knife,

 ③

   C G7   C   G7   C G7 C ⓪

Did you ever see such a sight in your life, as three blind mice?

   ④

Sweetly Sings The Donkey

D   / A7   D /   /   A7   D

Sweetly sings the donkey at the break of day;If you do not feed him, this is what he'll say,

①   ②

  D   /   A7   D

Hee - haw! Hee - haw! Hee - haw, hee - haw, hee - haw!

   ③

Frere Jacques

F /   /   /   /   /   /   /

Are you sleeping, are you sleeping, Brother John? Brother John?

①   ②

/   /   /   /   /   / /   /

Morning bells are ringing, morning bells are ringing, Ding, ding, dong, ding, ding, dong.

③   ④

Lovely Evening

D   / G D G D

Oh! How love-ly is the eve-ning, is the eve-ning,

①

D   / G D G D

When the bells are sweet-ly ring-ing, sweet-ly ring-ing,

②

D / G D G D

Ding, dong, ding, dong, ding, dong!

③

Hey, Ho! Nobody Home?

```
Gm Dm Gm      Dm  Gm     Dm      Gm        Dm
Hey, ho!  No - body home, Meat nor drink nor money have I none,
①                        ②
```

```
Gm  Dm    Gm Dm Gm Dm Gm        Dm
Yet I  will be mer - ry!  Hey, ho!  No - body home?
③                 ④
```

Vine and Fig Tree

```
        Dm          /     Gm     /         A7      /     Dm̄  /
And every man 'neath his vine and fig tree   shall live in peace and un—a—fraid,
①
```

```
        Dm          /     Gm     /         A7      /     Dm  /
And every man 'neath his vine and fig tree   shall live in peace and un—a—fraid.
```

```
Dm    /        Gm     /   A7     /     Dm     /
And into ploughshares turn their swords; Na—tions shall learn war no more,
②
```

```
Dm    /        Gm     /   A7     /     Dm     /
And into ploughshares turn their swords; Na—tions shall learn war no more.
```

I Love the Mountains

```
F      Dm    Gm     C7
I love the mountains, I love the rolling hills
①
```

```
F      Dm   Gm    C7
I love the flowers, I love the daffodils
②
```

```
F      Dm   Gm        C7
I love the fireside, when all the lights are low
③
```

```
F            Dm
Boom de ah dah, boom de ah dah,
④
```

```
Gm            C7
Boom de ah dah, boom de ah dah.
```

27

Scotland's Burning

```
C7          F       C7        F       C7    F  C7    F
```
Scotland's burning, Scotland's burning. Look out! Look out!
①   ②

```
C7   F   C7  F   C7      F       C7          F
```
Fire! Fire! Fire! Fire! Pour on wa - ter, pour on wa - ter.
③   ④

Kookaburra

```
C          F       C      /
```
Kookaburra sits on the old gum tree,
①

```
C            F       C      /
```
Mer - ry, mer - ry king of the bush is he;
②

```
C    F      C      /
```
Laugh, kookaburra, laugh, kookaburra,
③

```
C       F    C  /
```
Gay your life must be.
④

White Coral Bells

```
C   G7  C  /   F  G7    C   /
```
White coral bells up - on a slender stalk,
①

```
C   G7  C     /      F   G7 C  /
```
Lilies of the valley deck my gar - den walk.
②

```
C  G7     C  /  F       G7       C  /
```
Oh, don't you wish that you could hear them ring?
③

```
C       G7    C   /      F  G7 C
```
That will happen only when the fair - ies sing.
④

Cowboy Songs

Oh, Bury Me Not

F   / //   /   / //   /   **C7** //   /   **F** //
"Oh, bury me not — on the lone prai - rie," These words came low — and mournful - ly

  /   /   //   /   / //   /   **C7** //   /   **F** //
From the pallid lips — of a youth who lay   On his dying bed — at the close of day.

2. He'd wailed in pain — until o'er his brow Death's shadows fast — were gathering now
And he thought of home — and his loved ones nigh, As the cowboys came — there to see him die.

3. " How oft I remem — ber the well-known words Of the free wild — wind — and the songs of birds.
And I think of my cot—tage in the bower, And the friends I love — in my childhood's hour.

4. Oh, bury me not — on the lone prairie, Where the wild coyotes — will howl o'er me,
Where the rattlers hiss — and the crow flies free, oh, bury me not — on the lone prairie."

Goodbye, Old Paint

Chorus:
  D / /   /   //   **A7** /   /   **D**   /   / // /   //   **A7**   /   /   **D**   /
Good-bye, Old Paint, I'm a - leav - in' Chey - enne, good-bye, Old Paint, I'm a - leav - in' Chey - enne.

  D   / / /   /   / **A7** /   /   **D**   //   /   / /   / / /   / **A7**/   /   **D**   /
1. My foot's in the stir - rup, my po - ny won't stand. I'm a - leav - in' Chey - enne, I'm off to Mon - tan'. *Chorus*

2. I'm a - ridin' Old Paint, I'm a - leadin' Old Dan. Goodbye, little Annie, I'm a - leavin' Cheyenne. *Chorus*
3. Oh hitch up your horses and feed 'em some hay, And seat yourself by me as long as you stay. *Chorus*

Git Along Little Dogies

| C | F | G | C | / | | F | G7 | C |

As I was a - walkin' one morning for pleasure, I spied a young cow - puncher riding a - long.

| / | | F | G7 | C | / | F | G7 | C |

His hat was thrown back and his spurs were a - janglin, And as he ap - proached he was singing this song:

Chorus:

| G7 | / | C | / | G7 | / | C | / |

"Whoopee ti - yi - yo! Git a - long little dogies; it's your mis - fortune and none of my own.

| / | F | G | C | / | F | G7 | C |

Whoo - pee ti - yi - yo! Git a - long little dogies; you know that Wy - oming will be your new home."

2. It's early in the morning that we round up the dogies, We cut 'em and brand 'em and bob off their tails;
We hitch up the horses, load up the chuck wagon, Then throw the dogies out on the North Trail.

The Streets of Laredo

| F | C7 | F | C7 | F | C7 | F | C |

As I walked out on the streets of La - re - do, as I walked out in La - re - do one day,

| F | C7 | F | C7 | F | Gm | C7 | F |

I spied a young cow - boy all wrapped in white lin - en, all wrapped in white lin - en as cold as the clay.

2. " I see by your outfit that you are a cowboy," These words he did say as I boldly stepped by,
" Come sit down beside me and hear my sad story, I was shot in the chest and I know I must die."

3. " It was once in the saddle I used to go dashing, It was once in the saddle I worked hard all day,
At night to the dram - house and then to the card house. Got shot in the chest; I am dying today."

4. " Get six jolly cowboys to carry my coffin; Get six pretty maidens to carry my pall;
Put bunches of roses all over my coffin, Roses to deaden the clods as they fall."

5. We beat the drum slowly and played the fife lowly, And bitterly wept as we bore him along,
For we all loved our comrade, so brave, young, and handsome, We all loved our comrade, although he'd done wrong.

Red River Valley

F   /   /   C7 /   F   // /   / /   / /   C7   //
From this val - ley they say you are go - ing,   We will miss your bright eyes and sweet smile;

/   F /   F7 /   Bb   // / C7   /   /   /   F //
For they say you are tak - ing the sun - shine   That bright - ens our path - way a - while.

Refrain:
F   // /   C7 F   // /   / /   / /   C7 //
Come and sit by my side if you love me,   Do not hast - en to bid me a - dieu,

/   F /   (F7) /   Bb   // /   F   C7 /   F //
But re - mem - ber the Red Riv - er Val - ley,   And the girl that has loved you so true.

2. From this va - ley they say you are go - ing; When you go, may your dar - ling go, too?
Would you leave her be - hind un - pro - tect - ed When she loves no — oth - er but you?

3. As you go to your home by the o - cean, May you nev - er for - get those sweet hours
That we spent in the Red Riv - er Val - ley, And the love we ex - changed 'mid the flow'rs.

Old Texas (echo song)

F // /   /   //   /   C7 //   Bb   F //
I'm goin' to leave - old Texas now,   They've got no use — for the long - horn cow.

2. They've plowed and fenced — my cattle range, and the people there — are all so strange.
3. I'll take my horse, — I'll take my rope, and hit the trail — upon a lope.
4. Say adios — to the Alamo, and turn my head — toward Mexico.

Christmas Songs

Angels We Have Heard On High

```
F  /  Am /  C7 /  F  //     C7 F   /  /  C7    F    /
```
An - gels we have heard on high, Sweet - ly sing - ing o'er   the plains,

```
/   /  Am  /  C7 /   F  /  C7 /  /   F   C7   F   /
```
And the moun - tains in   re - ply,   E - cho - ing their joy - ous strains:

Refrain:
```
F  / D7 / Gm / C7 / F / B♭ / C  G7    C C7 F C7  F  B♭  F / C7 /
```
Glo- - - - - - - - - - - - - - - - ri - a,   In ex - cel - sis De - o,

```
F  / D7 / Gm / C7 / F / B♭ / C  G7    C C7 F C7  F  B♭  F / C7 / F
```
Glo- - - - - - - - - - - - - - - ri - a,   In ex - cel - sis De - - - - o.

2. Shepherds why this jubilee? Why your joyous strains prolong?
What the gladsome tiding be Which inspire your heavenly song? *Refrain*

Jingle Bells

```
F        /       / / /         /  B♭ / /     /       C7 / /     /    F  /
```
Dashing through the snow, in a one - horse open sleigh, O'er the fields we go,   laughing all the way;

```
F    /    / / /     /   B♭   /     / / C7     /  /     /      F  /
```
Bells on bobtail ring,   making spirits bright; What fun it is to ride, and sing a sleighing song to - night!

```
/   /   /   /   /  B♭  F / B♭    /  F /    G7         / C7   /
```
Jingle bells! Jingle bells! Jingle all the way!   Oh, what fun it is to ride in a one - horse open sleigh,

```
F  /   /   /   /  B♭  F / B♭    /  F /    C7         / F  /
```
Jingle bells! Jingle bells! Jingle all the way!   Oh, what fun it is to ride in a one - horse open sleigh.

Away In A Manger (first version)

```
C7 F   / / /   /   /   Bb  / /   F  C7  F /  C7  F /  /  /   /   G7   C7  /
```
A - way in a man-ger no crib for his bed, The lit-tle Lord Je - sus laid down his sweet head;

```
/  F   / / /   /  /  Bb  /     /  F  /  C7  F  /  C7  F  /  Bb  F   /  C7  F  /
```
The stars in the bright sky look down where he lay,   The lit - tle Lord Je - sus a - sleep on the hay.

2. The cat - tle are low - ing the poor ba - by wakes, But lit-tle Lord Je-sus no cry-ing he makes;
I love thee. Lord Je-sus, look down from the sky, And stay by my cra - dle 'till morn-ing is nigh.

Away In A Manger (second version)

```
C  F      /      Bb    F    C7     /      F            /
```
A - way in a manger, no crib for His bed, The little Lord Jesus laid down his sweet head;

```
/       /       Bb       F    C7     F    Bb    C7  F
```
The stars in the bright sky look down where he lay,   The little Lord Jesus a - sleep in the hay.

2. The cattle are lowing the poor baby wakes, But little Lord Jesus, no crying he makes.
I love thee, Lord Jesus, look down from the sky, And stay by my cradle 'till morning is nigh.

Deck The Halls With Boughs Of Holly

```
C       /       /       /  G7     C     / G7 C
```
Deck the halls with boughs of holly, fa la la la la — la la la la!

```
/       /       /   /  G7      C     / G7 C
```
'Tis the season to be jolly, fa la la la la — la la la la!

```
G7      /     C    /     /     Am       G D7 G
```
Don we now our gay ap-par -el, fa la la – la la la — la la la!

```
C       /       /       /    F      C    F C G7 C
```
Troll the an -cient yule -tide car-ol, fa la la la la — la la la la!

Jolly Old Saint Nicholas

F   /   C7   / Dm   /   Am / Bb   /   F   / G7   /   C7 /
Jolly old Saint Nicho - las, lean your ear this way;   Don't you tell a single soul, what I'm goin' to say;

F   /   C7   /   Dm   /   Am / Bb   /   F   / C7   / F /
Christmas eve is coming soon. Now you dear old man,   Whisper what you'll bring to me; Tell me if you can.

I Saw Three Ships

F   C7   F   C7 F   /   C7   /
I saw three ships come sailing in, on Christmas day, on Christmas day,

F   C7   F   C7 F   /   C7   F
I saw three ships come sailing in, on Christmas day in the morn - ing.

2. Pray, whither sailed those ships all three, on Christmas day, on Christmas day?
Pray, whither sailed those ships all three, on Christmas day in the morning?

3. 0, they sailed into Bethlehem, on Christmas day, on Christmas day;
0, they sailed into Bethlehem, on Christmas day in the morning.

4. And what was in those ships all three, on Christmas day, on Christmas day?
Oh, what was in those ships all three, on Christmas day in the morning?

5. So, let us all rejoice again, on Christmas day, on Christmas day;
So, let us all rejoice again, on Christmas day in the morning

---

Silent Night

C F C /   / F C /   G7 / /   C / / C7 F   /   / G7 F C   F C   /
Si - lent night, ho - ly night, all is calm, all is bright.   Round yon Vir - gin Moth - er and Child,

F   / /   G7 F C F C /   G7 / /   /   / C / /   / / G7   /   / C
Ho - ly In - fant so ten - der and mild, Sleep in heav - en - ly peace. Sle - ep in heav - en - ly peace.

We Three Kings Of Orient Are

```
Dm        /       A7  Dm  /      /       A7      Dm
```
We three kings of Orient are, bearing gifts we traverse a - far,

```
/        C       F       /       Gm      Dm  A7 Dm
```
Field and fountain, moor and mountain, following yon - der star.

```
C7 / F    /       B♭  F   /      /       B♭      F
```
0, — star of wonder, star of night, star of royal beauty bright,

```
Dm    C     B♭     C       F       /       B♭      F
```
Westward leading, still pro - ceed - ing, guide us to thy per - fect light.

Children Go (cumulative song)

Refrain:
```
F       / /     /       /
```
Children go where I send thee;

```
/   /   /       /
```
How shall I send thee?

```
/       /       /       /
```
1. I'm gonna' send thee one by one,

```
/       /       /   /
```
One for the little bitty ba - by,

```
/   / B♭ / F     C7      F
```
That's born - born - born in Beth - le - hem.

2. *Refrain* I'm gonna' send thee two by two, two for Mary and Joseph. (Repeat 1st verse.)
3. *Refrain* Three for the three old - wise men. (Repeat 2nd verse, then 1st verse, and continue in this manner.)
4. *Refrain* Four for the four who stood at the door.
5. *Refrain* Five for the Hebrew - children.
6. *Refrain* Six for the six who didn't get fixed.
7. *Refrain* Seven for the seven who went to heaven.

Oh, Come, All Ye Faithful (Adeste Fideles)

```
F   / /   / /  C7 /   // F    C7 F  Bb   F  /  C7
```
Oh, come, all ye faith - ful, joy - ful and tri - um - phant,

```
Dm  / G7 C  G7  C G7 C  F C / G7 /     C /  C7 /
```
Oh, come ye, oh, come ye to Beth - le - hem.

```
F  /   C7 F   Bb  C7 F  /  C    A7 Dm  G7 C / G7 C
```
Come and be - hold   Him born the King of an - gels

```
F  /    C  F C7 F / /   /  /   C F  Bb F  /  C
```
Oh, come, let us a - dore Him, oh, come, let us a - dore Him,

```
F   Bb    F  C  Dm C7 / Dm Gm  F / C7 /     F  //
```
Oh, come, let us a - dore   Him,   Christ   the Lord.

2. Sing, choirs of angels, sing in exultation,
Oh, sing, all ye citizens of heaven above.
Glory to God, all glory in the highest;
Oh, come, let us adore Him, Oh, come, let us adore Him,
Oh, come, let us adore Him, Christ, the Lord!

The First Noel

```
G7  C  Am G F G7 C  G   F  C   F  G7 C  G  F   C    F   G7 C    / G7  C
```
The first No - el the   an - gels did say, Was to cer - tain poor shep - herds in fields as they lay.

```
G7 C    Am  G  F G7 C   G  F  C      F G7 C  G    F   C F G7 C / G7 C
```
In fields where they lay   keep - ing their sheep, On a   cold win - ter's night that was so deep.

```
G7  C Am G  C   F  /   C  Am G F  C F G7 C / G7 C
```
No - el. No - el. No - el. No - el. Born is the King of Is - ra - el.

Pat-a-Pan (French)

```
Gm    /      /      /         Cm      Gm /  D7
```
Willie take your lit - tle drum, Robin bring your fife and come,

Chorus:
```
D7    /      /      Gm   /             / D7              /
```
Playing on your fife and drum, too - re - loo - re - lu, pat - a - pat - a - pan

```
/      /      /      Gm      Cm      D7  / Gm
```
We'll make music loud and gay for our Christmas hol - i - day.

2. Shepherds glad in ancient days gave the King of Kings their praise. *Chorus*
3. Christian men rejoice as one, leave your work and join our fun. *Chorus*

Bring A Torch, Jeannette Isabella

```
F     Dm      Gm    C7   F     Dm      Gm C7 F
```
Bring a torch, Jean - nette Isa - bel - la, Bring a torch to the cra - dle run.

```
/  /         /       C     Bb    F      Gm    C7
```
It is Jesus, good folk of the village, Christ is born, and Mary's call - ing;

```
Dm C F      C    F    A7 Dm C F      Gm C7 F
```
Ah, ah, beautiful is the mo - ther, Ah, ah, beautiful is   the child.

2. It is wrong when the child is sleeping, It is wrong to talk so loud.
Silence, all, as you gather around, Lest — your noise should waken Jesus:
Hush! Hush! See how fast he slumbers. Hush! Hush! See how fast he sleeps.

3. Softly to the little stable, Softly for a moment come!
Look and see how charming is Jesus, How He is bright, His cheeks are rosy!
Hush! Hush! See how the child is sleeping. Hush! Hush! See how He smiles in dreams.

The Wassail Song

```
C        /        /          /
Here we come a - was - sail - ing

       /       .  /        /      /
A - mong the leaves so green;

 F       C       /  Dm      /  /  G7
Here we come a - wan - d'ring so fair to be seen
```

Refrain:
```
C        /  F       C
Love and joy come to you

 /       /       F      C
And to you, your wassail too,

 /        /   A7       Dm  G7
And God bless you, and send you

  C       /       F
A Hap - py New Year,

C        /  A7  Dm  G7       C
And God send you a Hap - py New Year!
```

2. We are not daily beggars
That beg from door to door;
But we are neighbors children,
Whom you have seen before. *Refrain*

3. God bless the master of this house,
Likewise the mistress, too,
And all the little children,
That round the table go. *Refrain*

We Wish You a Merry Christmas

C7 F /   /   Bb   /   / G7 /   /   C7   /
We wish you a merry Christ - mas, We wish you a merry Christ - mas,

/ A7 /   /   Dm   /   F   Bb Gm C7   F
We wish you a merry Christ - mas, And a Hap - py New Year.

Refrain:
C7 F /   / C   / F C G7 C   /   F C F C   / F   Gm / C7 F
Good tid - ings we bring to you and your friends; Good tid - ings for Christ - mas and a Hap - py New Year.

2. Now bring us a figgy pudding *(repeat three times)* and bring it right here.
3. We won't go until we get some *(repeat three times)* so bring it right now.

Up On The Housetop

C   /   /   /
Up on the housetop the reindeer pause,

F   C   G7   /
Out jumps good old Santa Claus,

C   /   /   /
Down through the chimney with lots of toys

F   C   G7   C
All for the little ones Christmas joys.

Chorus:
F   / C   / G7   / C   /
Ho, Ho, Ho! Who wouldn't go! Ho, Ho, Ho! Who wouldn't go!

/   /   F   / C   /   G7   C
Up on the housetop click, click, click, Down through the chimney with good St. Nick.

2. First comes the stocking of little Nell, oh, dear Santa, fill it well.
Give her a dolly that laughs and cries, one that can open and shut its eyes. *Chorus*

3. Next, comes the stocking of little Will; oh, just see what a glorious fill!
Here is a hammer and lots of tacks, also a ball and a whip that cracks. *Chorus*